The Curse of Prometheus 1994

Stephen W. Sweigart

Paperback: 978-1-953731-78-4
eBook: 978-1-953731-77-7
Library of Congress Control Number: 2020924077

This is a work of fiction

Ordering Information:

BookTrail Agency
8838 Sleepy Hollow Rd.
Kansas City, MO 64114

Printed in the United States of America

THE MARTYRDOM:
THE REVENGE OF ART

DOWER TWELFE

THE CHARACTERS OF REALITY

PROMETHEUS	
EPIMETHEUS	
PANDORA	ATHENE
DELUSIVE HOPE	
OLD AGE	
LABOUR	
SICKNESS	
INSANITY	
VICE	FALSEHOOD
PASSION	

1 Vexillator

Hello! I am a homeless person.
I am doing an experiment, on the ability,
Of
HOMO SAPIENS
To survive in a world of
Evolved
HETRO SAPIENS.
Unfortunately , I am also an employee
Of the famed FIBbers. I am a devout Christian
And as the poet, Sebastian, has written.
The new Mole (code language) must prove that
I am FIBber.
People have began to assert that we were all dissemblers
And that our theology never worked at all.
Well, I myself do not accept theology, I am
Fundamental. Since Hume proved the nonexistence
Of God, and another mad man, declared
His
Death.
THE DIRECTOR
Was set up, by the first
Women lesbian litigant in command.
She was also programmed, by Sebastian;
I curse the day of his birth, Magog, my God!
Save us, it was all planned. Forgive us.
I am told since we have blockaded the Marxist,
And mankind has become atheist.
That we will all become homeless. My God, we have sinned
We have starved people in the name of Jesus.
So now in order to earn food, I must continue with
This experiment that we too will survive. Thank You.

2. Vexilator.

ZEUS had revealed to us the secret affair.
PROMETHEUS went past the warrant, and
Was not to save mankind, amused LUST and FILTH.
He had also been seen with a PROSTITUTE, named
JULIETTA. Once a nun, she was pious, so many
Times that she prayed, to succeed, to save religion
From insolvency. PROMETHEUS slipped in through her
And obtained the great fire from the SUN.
ZEUS then created PANDORA, a women out of porcelain,
The most resplendent and beautiful of all creatures.
PROMETHEUS who had been chained to a rock after
His affair with JULIETTA, escaped and claimed
That he had jarred all the destructive forces,
That might damage THE GROWTH OF MANKIND.
The great fire had been released and mankind freed.
Now, good neighbors, THE PLAGUE IS FREE.
Rejoice! Rejoice! Mankind will eat raw meat.

THE DIRECTOR OF THE NATION {on a skafold of Politik}

And what is THE CURSE OF PROMETHEUS?
Who is PROMETHEUS? And who is ZEUS?
What is Mythology, and what is Poetry?
POETRY IS NOTHING, nothing sells.
I AM A CAPITALIST, A LEADER IN COMMERCE.
This is all a nuisance, and now I have
Discovered this person has written,
And understands correctly, what we are.
This is obscene, men talk of War;
I repeat, I AM A CHRISTIAN, this is a maxim.
I have been voted into power, and
Everyone knows I am a gentle person.
My wife is the first women allowed
To sell cookies in THE WHITE PALACE
Formerly McKee D's. we have confined
Many people to rid us of these non-eco
People. TAXES taketh from the poor.
Time Out! THE COWBOYS are about to score!

PANDORA {on the skafold of the World}

EPIMETHEUS, the brother of Prometheus
Has rejected me, a gift from THE DIRECTOR.
ZEUS has revenged and chained manhood
I have come to life, as mere clay, in
The winds of the autumn rain and floods
Of flakes that drift. Now revenged at
Last. Zeus must fence off the myth of
HEAVEN. I am PANDORA, the new creation.
The most beautiful of women. Far above
The goddesses of heaven. Whom must adore,
My excellence. SCIENCE is my escort
The pillar of advancement. MANKIND
Is THE CURSE, my creator must bear?
Why must I be barren? Why must
I suffer the fate abandoned?
My MUSE will avenge me, life
Will resume, but for now NON-BEING!

EPIMETHEUS

My brother, PROMETHEUS, has begged me
To be careful and not accept any gift
From THE DIRECTOR. It would be unwise
To insult Zeus. PROMETHEUS has been
The arbitrator and tricked him into
Accepting the divine portion. Deceived
And laughed at, he withheld the fire
From mankind.

My brother now chained had awakened
Me and I must accept the offering laid
Before my feet. I have married PANDORA
To advert my own fate. However foolish
And senseless she may be, ZEUS, is more
Powerful than a Titan. FALSEHOOD and
RUMOR are the methods of THE DIRECTOR.
ATHENE has never soiled his lips, as
A soldier, she is THE GODDESS OF WISDOM,
And CRAFTS. He has entered by her and…

ATHENE {on a skafold of the Heavens}

The ALIENIST desires to enter PROMETHEUS;
Espial as a portion of ZEUS'S reign.
Thought control is his method, Word Choice
Is mimicked guess techniques. The DIRECTOR
In the crown of heaven appears and
Espouses your FREE CHOICE. FREEDOM
Is this guy's will, THE WILL OF HEAVEN.

Mankind is what? An ANOPNPOS? I like
The form, excuses me, the door is rapped.
PROMETHEUS it is you! I was fixing my hair
And dream of riches that the GODS offer.
DARLING your reason for entering?
This is the reason I know you are now SANE!
But you were not this way before. DARLING.

DELUSIVE HOPE

They have a CORPORATION for production of information.
At the computer sits the former conspirer, PARNASSIA.
The She-Communication-Propagandist would no longer visit
The Balaton. PROMETHEA who was recently elected to
The consul of the Deities, regretted the loss of financiers,
Had begun PRIVITIZATION and the INDIVIDUALIZATION.
There investments would be irredeemable if the Deutsch
Would be permitted to occupy the vacation area. Sebastian
Returned to PRAHA promptly, the day after the demonstrations
Re-elected an old government. This had been foretold years
Before in THE CASTLE MUSEUM. Now they would be free again,
The political patricians would better themselves even if they
Had HALLUCINATIONS.

Komrade lAvel's relative told me of how he had attempted
To make public the written theories of his new finances.
Mr. wAdar had published his speeches, and Mistress lvel
Wished to show the world that his region would DISTRIBUTE.
These theories which he had contributed in the former
Local jazz club, before THE AMERICANS had returned
Regional 'rock' and popular 'ELECTRONIC' music.
He convinced THE LEADERSHIP that the Americans had indeed
Invented 'rock and roll' and that this was only legal
And would destroy all INTERNATIONAL ORDER. The Sofiet
Leaders thought this of minor importance to have
And international crisis over the music of the dissident,
WHITE TRASH.

The capitalist laughed that this fool in the Sofiet leadership
had such a good heart that he believed that all religious people
were like his grandmother.

PROMETHEUS

I will not accept ZEUS position.
I have deceived THE DIRECTOR, his
Preference, skeleton and lard, and
His VENGENCE for distaste of Man.
From you, ATHENE, sweet child I
Have learned what was expelled.
THE ARTS, and SCIENCES from his
Crown.

The servile judge from the heavens
Has decreed that MANKIND is unfit,
And we must be rid of their kind.
Zeus has refused to permit Fire
From the CHARIOT OF HEAVEN, I must
Ignite and deliver the flame from
This SUN. Thank you, my dear,
Now I will repay your favor.

SICKNESS {oN a Skafold of Mal{ice}.

I AM A CHRISTIAN, A JEW, AND A CATHOLIC.
I AM SICKNESS. I have varnished man's nature
I deteriorate his body, weaken it.
Vomit, I am NAUSEA and pain is my sorrow.
Joy is my heart, sadism my mortality.
Disappointment ruins our intestines, infest
With microorganisms, my spine, my brain.
Pastel pale is my color, menstrual, my tint.
SELFLESSNESS for belief in this gild religion.
True faith is our ultimate treasure, our idol.
We are DISEASED, we are pretty, or riffraff.

I AM AILING, since my operation I have not been
Well. They have now a new name, to recreate new
Funds. IMMUNITY and PREPETUATION enhance WEALTH.
We can afford to dissect, to ATATOMIZE your Creed.
We can assure you of worst health. Your AGENT has
Contacted us, you are in fine hands with us too.
Your MINISTER has also called, the driver of the VEHICLE
Was KILLED. I have been not informed of this until
Your release. The new leader of the government
Needs samples of your blood type, your URINE,
And a specimen of ejaculation; no; discharge,
Is the present polite phrase. PRESIDENT GORBAKN
Has not ordered this, the new leader will.

Your BEHAVIOR has caused this tragic accident, this
Statement is designed, by the SENATOR, to test your
Loyalty, but I was asleep and I don't remember.
Was I this person? Was I in an accident, was this
My doing. My God! Magog! MR. SCRUB was murdered,
And he is free. He has never harmed anyone.
He broke every LAW OF GOOD MANNERS.
I was the daughter of a physician,
It is not possible to be ERRATA.

INSANITY

These are my INSTRUMENTS: bribery, and slander.
We dissect insight, knowledge and replace it,
With experience; labor, idleness, slumber,
Sabotage, ignorance, mimicry, postulation,
Edginess, presumption, and misperception.
WE SURROUND ourselves with mouths, teeth,
Hair, silence, smell, disease, viruses,
Germs, filth, reconstruction, fibers,
Used-machinery, voiceless speech,
Whining and idiocy.

LAWS are dollars, poverty is status,
Judgement is hearing, harassment, homicide,
Vice, riches are debt, wealth money. TIME
A journal, propaganda sheet, entertainment,
Liquor, smoke, nausea, aspirins, deterioration,
Strength, medicine, abstinence, prohibition,
Rights, violation of self, treaties, agreements,
Poisons, mindlessness, destruction, boldness,
Dirt, exile, homelessness, debate, legislation,
Candor, deception, filibuster, film, and incest.

I am REGROWTH; premature ripeness; frigidness;
Stillness, regression, triumph, involvement.
I was a MONARCH; a leper; regeneration, and
Instruction. You are espial, attendance, and
Enthusiasm, gazing, reporting, mediation,
participation, worship, listening, yet realization.

You got it, PROMETHEUS is old fashion,
And before my parents speak, OLD AGE
Will climb the skafold; so for now
And a little later TELEMANN. Bring
Forth the legislation.
The poet never completed this poem
And was tortured into writing PROMETHEUS.
I had hope to fool him, but he has spoken
To me, his confident, that this poem

Is ENVIRONMENTAL. The poet has control
Of the district, he has been there a few
Times; and he is very liberal, you know
He doesn't permit anyone to do anything
Productive. So he has put this aside
And the FOURTEENTH VENGENCE
is warming up.

FINALLY, THAT famed portion, which lead
the poet near the state of permanent
exaltation. Why not spend a little time
in the barracks? Why fight for Poetry, he
has reminded us? MY GODDESS, fight for
the politik; For if religions
are good, POETRY IS GREATER, all that is
right, all that is unjust, all else is crime.

DIRECTOR! Politiks is vulgar,
A prerequisite
For the accumulation of wealth.
Necessary, for the regression
Of the PARNASSIAN homeland,
The nameless fatherland.

So the poet,
Set aside this great work,
Which someday he will return to,
I am sure. For now, be illuminated
That we will alter his imprint!
Get ready, THE FOURTEENTH appearith.
A former English Maidenhead.
Thank you, Thank you.

The skafold of Mal{ice}.

We are not old, we are OLD AGE.
Weakness and power command.
Our voice is not heard, yet
when we speak meaninglessness
become the defense of others.

Pretenders and felons
Announce and emulate their preconception
While they rationa_ize their notions.
Their lack of feelings.

MORANS MINIC

Discussion and debate,

simulate advertisement.

While we rest and concern ourselves

With pastimes and contemplation.

Their plans and our diversions,

their manipulations, extortion's, and blackmails

frighten the past, and our trivial intents.

We relive and remake, preventing

creations. How may we prolong life?

May we be awakened into quietness

And serenity or stirred into discontent quietude?

May we not sleep or be crushed beneath

our marrow!

May we not frailly conceive nightmares of possessions.
TIME must be made present, the end must be enlightened
And seen, passed on. pushed forward.
STIFLED!

After years of similitude   and habitual manner
hindsight conquers and   perpetuates the estate
against political and   grins us into boredom
from distractions.
EXCITEMENT in tranquility   and exultation, frenzy
ADICTION TO ACHIEVEMENT   AND COMMUNITY
PROPAGATION.

Oneness and power tyrannize   and UPLIFT minute
distinctions.
commands and childish dances
grow into fashion with them
enliven and perpetuated   forgotten relived restrengthen.

Youth empowered by us,   old age, not stifled or
hindered. We no longer   conduct or orchestrate,
we construct, reorganize,
replace, and resent   observation, learning.

Contribute to control   and destroy
so political arrant
can render wastefulness   productive
disruptions   and violence
to render potholes   of red tape
and experiments   impolitely

HOSIPITALS threaten us,
and torture our children
ruin our saving,
squandering lielessness.

We still perform our daily chores and perceive
what we are told and imagine PROMISES fulfilled
enlivened
buried in dependence and re-enlightened northward
inherited.

The grand cities anointed and suppression at
stimulation.

The remembrances of our forefathers revealed in silence
secrets not revealed emotions risen and repeated daily.

When will we guess or desire immorality perpetuated
profit?

We could offer an ELIXIR in health perpetuated in
insight
thrills and chill our souls. neo-spirits, non-beings
striving in flesh to ignore any paradise or heaven.
merely to mend a button, or clean a dish, forever
is drugged stimulation of repeated observation.

There are no spirits and ghost only lifelessness
transcended in mind process
and thoughts. We will no longer be old age
we will hide forever! We will be forgotten, lost,
disbanded,
but may return to this theme, yet we are OLD AGE.
There is no eternity or afterlife we are OLD AGE.
We rule while others reign in triumph and
succession.

FALSEHOOD

Today my follows, I have   heard falsehood.
As I was at the shopping mall,
an agent of falsity was silent
She is the MINISTER OF INQUIRY.
He is in manservant against   the law
He defies the unimaginative,   they summons
liberty of thought reading.   she submits
ANNOYANCE diverts his attraction,
He lust without feeling or   involvement
Now a pamphlet of marcescent   has been published

People walk the streets in pairs,   another man
plods along the sidewalk,
two women chat
I have forgotten what it is like   to be a host
to worship my citizens, I remember   once I was in old age,
once I was in sickness. the world   abandon me not
it was at my shelter, my pleasure.   my clothing
ruined.

THE ARENA OF MARS: a junk car,   a red chariot.

a file neglected, Yet I was not   in the present,
nor the past, hereafter.
I am not the author of this rhyme,   these creatures
are salvation, for now I will   live forever.
That I remembered the hope   that I will return.
DEATH has been defeated,   Falsehood reigns; transformation
into Vice

You have forgotten, I spoke to myself,   our ministry observes a woman.

[descending the skafold:] [Passion ascends the Banns…]
From above the heavens, we hear the underworld.
We have demolished and wrecked; Let us return to those
Words which you, my parishioners, were conceived without…

LABOUR [skafold of the world]

Last night I was raw from EXPERIMENTATION,
For twenty years I have not been able to practice
My profession. Wages are my accumulation of PRIVACY.
Everything is a lie, the hope of opportunity bestowed
Upon the advantaged, those who are fortunate to believe
Work without a profession. I myself have followed the path
of the yard, which I have purchased. I am weary of servitude.
I have escaped the mule road of RELIGION, and the highway
CAPITALISM. Now I lay in a chair and relax and study...

I receive the appreciation of happiness, the enemy that
Prays upon generation, and tortures everyone, robs them. This
Is servitude, the HOSPITAL of the martyred COMMANDER. The
Demonic hideous PHANTOMS, the morbid methods of MECHANICS.

HEALTH is their knowledge, LOVE learning, death their TENDER,
Raw words and bribery, stupidity and misinformation; their food
Poison, torn clothing; dollars paper, and false collection.
TV (television), sports, drugs, liquor, medicines, magazines,
Preconceived mental perversions, a decrepit community.
Whose correctness is inhumanity. Yet I LABOR, am not their employer
Neither correctness is INHUMANITY. I LABOR, the tool of their
Inoculation.

THE DIRECTOR OF THE NATION desires a robust environment
He has switched health care supplements

After a reign of chaos, it has taken us one year
To enact our program, fairness for your generation.
I have informed my press, at our latest conference.
That we will lift the embargo on our brethren in the high land.
There the palm trees create warm weather and dry snow.
THE DIRECTOR OF HE STATE

An actor attempted to enter the home of the great Imposter!
As usually he was loaded, smoked legal methane; and had
OLD AGE with children and potato chips; he also solicited
The fired and disgraced writer; of course, this is established
That he can neither write or spell or read; Jeef s his name.
JEEF dragged to infiltrate the atmosphere, to sanctity the new
Electrical system as the promotion plugger, labored a weapon
Fruitfully for the return of heroine of the NATION.

In disguise, as usual, she was accosted by intruders
She would of course reveal to the community the enlightened
Opinion of Jeef's mother's OBSESSION. Her dear son
Would one day save the community of violence and
Terrorism. The Jeef would not permit this and began
An alinement to incarcerate this perpetuator
Of world tranquility. The town failed to relocate
Five dollars paid for Jeef's next visitation; January
Proved profitable toward the attainment of the sought
For elimination of unrest,

Years of improvement by out ladies in the fifties building
Proved deteriorating to the determent of the SIA; unfortunate.

He had not been permited to restrict his dogs to the location
Therefore, the though the elks in New Jerzip, repair the
Azinc-layer, as depicted in the flop film which Sfed
Imitated about failed impersonators guardian.

Demolition by prayer of the building.

The jar

My words kill this person who ordered the alteration of this speech.

PASSION

And you have slept, and not liked?
My avidity in you, now you do not?
PROMETHEUS, I do not shape your appeals
I do not speak? You must! I use you? No.
We memorized this automobile on decapitalized tv
We now must do this, unlike them, at leisure.
they will never overturn our fraternization.
For what good is it to me; I have now learned
This from TV. You father, ZEUS, told you of this.
We women; PROMETHEUS, we have no passion.
Only PLEASURE. I will try this on you: you like this.

Yes, perhaps yes, what is your name? Spell what?
Speak what? Don't talk, you like this. Why do you
Not finish. PASSION, why do you not finish?
Is it too much for you? SWEETWOMEN, it is not!
Why do you turn your neck; is not your neck more?
Beautiful? No, don't turn. Do smile. Foe ATHENE
Loves me, and hates you. Yes. Now do you JUSTITA,
Please.

Why answer you? Figure it out, look at me, look at me.
Why must I look at you? Must I touch you? Will you slit
Their wrist. My pleasure? Will you? Now you are fine.
My veins feel better, your bust, feel on palms
Teach me, how you like it. Will you stay, before FOURTEEN.
My birthday is tomorrow, will you stay? Will you.

No, I must? not. This is passion. You are pleasurable.
PASSION. I must be in Sophia. In FOURTEEN. Then to home?
Yes, then to VENGENCE. Call me. Why not finish? Why not finish?
My number, paper, write. Call me. Finish, Return when?
For police, protection, money? Please to Sophia.
Problem. Pleasure. I go. I finish. No pay me.

VICE

My name is VICE. It is a nice name.
The religious slander me. I am a nice
Figure. VICE is the means with which
POETRY, and it's immortal increment
Pulchritudian Parnassian EPOETEST
Eminent and eliminate the virtues
Of the illiterate. Prostitution
Is my finest virtue. Buffoonery
Is my second, I love only
Self-indulgence, I only deprive
The religious of this marriage.
For their corruption is donation,
Contribution. I am fine, I am good.
I am best. I don't wish to propagate.
I wish to wed. I like enjoyment,
Celebrity. I am, THE VICEROY of PLEASURE.
The initiator of PASSION, the creator
Of theology: the employment of ethics.

CPSIA information can be obtained
at www.ICGtesting.com
Printed in the USA
LVHW040050140323
741536LV00026B/1465

9 781953 731784